Fast Facts About
CORGIS

by Marcie Aboff

PEBBLE
a capstone imprint

Pebble Emerge is published by Pebble, an imprint of Capstone.
1710 Roe Crest Drive
North Mankato, Minnesota 56003
www.capstonepub.com

**Library of Congress Cataloging-in-Publication Data is available on the Library
of Congress website.**
ISBN 978-1-9771-2455-5 (library binding)
ISBN 978-1-9771-2498-2 (eBook PDF)

Summary: Calling all corgi fans! Ever wondered about a corgi's personality? Want
to find out the best way to care for this type of dog? Kids will learn all about corgis
with fun facts, beautiful photos, and an activity.

Image Credits
Capstone Press/Karon Dubke, 20: Getty Images/STF/Staff, 18; iStockphoto/
fotografixx, 5; Shutterstock: Bulltus_Casso, backcover, eAlisa, 8, Happy monkey,
cover, 11, 16, hd connelly, cover (right), Masarik, 4, 17, Nadezhda V. Kulagina,
10, Nejron Photo, 15, Pavel Shlykov, 6, Sarit Richarson, 9, Sergey Lavrentev, 13,
TatyanaPanova, 7

Artistic elements: Shutterstock: Anbel, Ponysaurus

Editorial Credits
Editor: Megan Peterson; Designer: Sarah Bennett; Media Researcher: Kelly Garvin;
Production Specialist: Tori Abraham

All internet sites appearing in back matter were available and accurate when this
book was sent to press.

Printed in the United States of America.
3342

Table of Contents

Words in **bold** are in the glossary.

Small and Mighty Corgis

Corgis are small and mighty dogs. They are lively and active. They can be bold too. Corgis are small dogs that sometimes act like big dogs!

Corgis have a kind face. They are also smart. They like to learn. Corgis make happy and loving pets. Families love these loyal, playful dogs.

Corgis have short, strong legs. They have a long back. Puppies have floppy ears. Their ears stand up as they grow. Corgis stand 10 to 12 inches (25 to 30 centimeters) tall. They weigh up to 30 pounds (13.6 kilograms).

A corgi's fur can be **sable**, red, or black and tan. Some can also have white marks. Corgis have a **double coat**. The topcoat is longer. It can be fluffy. The bottom coat is shorter. Their fur keeps them warm.

Corgi History

The first corgis came from Wales hundreds of years ago. They **herded** cattle and sheep. Corgis nipped at the animals' heels! This made the sheep and cattle move.

Corgis came to the United States in the 1900s. Families grew to love these brave, friendly dogs. Today, they are part of the herding group of dogs. Some run and jump in contests. Corgis are one of the most popular dog **breeds**.

Corgis at Home

Corgis are happy living in a small apartment or a big house. They are gentle with children. They get along well with other pets. Don't leave them alone too long. They want to be with their family!

Corgis make good watchdogs. These small dogs have a big bark! They will bark at strangers. Corgis want to keep their owners safe. They are not afraid.

Corgis are fast dogs with a lot of **energy**. They love running and jumping in dog contests.

Corgis need daily **exercise**. Let your corgi run around a track. Take it on long walks or short jogs. Give your corgi plenty of fresh water after.

Keeping Corgis Healthy

Corgis are usually healthy dogs. They can have eye and hip problems. Corgis need to visit the **veterinarian** every year. The vet will check the dog's eyes and hips. They will also check the heart, ears, and lungs. Corgis live about 12 to 13 years.

Caring for a Corgi

Corgis are eager to train. Sometimes they want their own way! Be firm but kind with corgis. Then they will listen. Puppies will learn to behave.

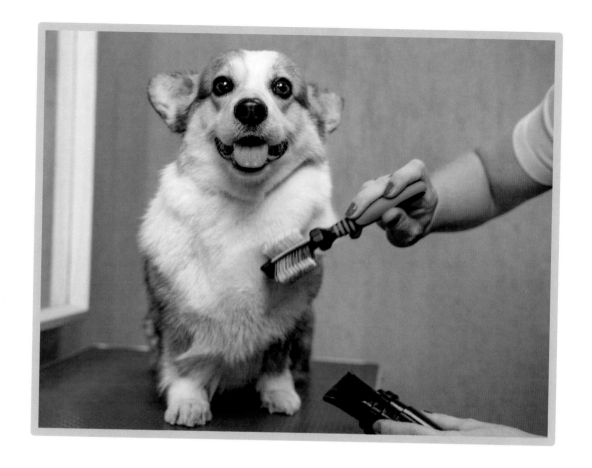

Corgis **shed** a lot of fur. They should be brushed daily. Corgis usually don't get too dirty. Bathe them as needed. Brush their teeth with dog toothpaste. And don't overfeed a corgi. They sometimes eat too much!

Fun Facts About Corgis

- Queen Elizabeth II of England loves corgis.
  She has owned more than 30 corgis!

- Corgi means "dwarf dog" in Welsh.

- A corgi party is held in California every year. More than 1,000 corgis gather together at one time!

- A Welsh **fairy tale** says corgis once pulled carriages for fairies.

- Some corgis are born without tails.

Frozen Sock Toy

What You Need:

- two long socks
- water
- freezer

What You Do:

1. Lay two socks on top of each other. Place the open ends together. Place the closed ends together.

2. Starting at the closed end, roll the socks up together.

3. Grab the open end of the outer sock. Wrap it around the entire sock roll.

4. Soak the sock toy in water. Place the sock toy in the freezer for about two hours.

5. Give the sock to your corgi to chew outside!

Glossary

breed (BREED)—a certain kind of animal within an animal group

double coat (DUH-buhl KOHT)—a coat that is thick and soft close to the skin and covered with lighter, silky fur on the surface

energy (EH-nuhr-jee)—the strength to do active things without getting tired

exercise (EK-suhr-syz)—physical activity done in order to stay healthy and fit

fairy tale (FAYR-ee TAIL)—a simple, magical story

herd (HURD)—to round up animals, such as sheep, and keep them together

sable (SAY-buhl)—tan hairs with black or brown ends

shed (SHED)—to lose hair

veterinarian (vet-ur-uh-NAYR-ee-uhn)—a doctor trained to take care of animals

Read More

Bozzo, Linda. *I Like Corgis!* New York: Enslow Publishing, 2017.

Leighton, Christina. *Pembroke Welsh Corgis.* Minneapolis: Bellwether Media, Inc., 2017.

Ransom, Candice. *Pembroke Welsh Corgis.* Minneapolis: Lerner Publications, 2019.

Internet Sites

American Kennel Club
https://www.akc.org/dog-breeds/pembroke-welsh-corgi/

Animal Planet
http://www.animalplanet.com/breed-selector/dog-breeds/herding/pembroke-welsh-corgi.html

Dogtime
https://dogtime.com/dog-breeds/pembroke-welsh-corgi#/slide/1

Index